KIDNAP

Badger Publishing Limited, Oldmedow Road, Hardwick Industrial Estate, King's Lynn PE30 4JJ
Telephone: 01438 791037

www.badgerlearning.co.uk

KIDNAP

TOMMY DONBAVAND

Kidnap ISBN 978-1-78147-571-3

Text © Tommy Donbavand 2014
Complete work © Badger Publishing Limited 2014

Publisher: Susan Ross
Senior Editor: Danny Pearson
Copyeditor: Cheryl Lanyon
Designer: Bigtop Design Ltd
Printed by Bell and Bain Ltd, Glasgow

2 4 6 8 10 9 7 5 3

CHAPTER 1

SHOPPING LIST

I could feel the security guard's eyes burning into the back of my neck. He'd been following me around the supermarket for the past ten minutes or so, convinced I was up to no good.

He didn't know the half of it.

I stopped in the cheese aisle and picked up two blocks of cheddar from the shelf, holding one behind the other. Studying the label on the front block, I shook my head slightly to demonstrate that wasn't what I was looking for – then I replaced the back block on the shelf, while sliding the front block up the fraying sleeve of my jumper.

I continued down the aisle, casually lowered my arm down to my side and caught the hidden block of cheddar with my fingers. Then I reached into my bag for my shopping list and swiftly dropped the cheese inside.

Cheese on toast for tea tonight, then.

I was proud of this bag. The best one I'd built in ages. It was made of a stiff material that didn't shake too much when I dropped things into it, and it was completely lined with tin foil to stop security tags from setting off the supermarket's alarms when I was ready to leave. That was just as well, as I already had two mobile phones, a handful of DVDs, a jar of pasta sauce and a loaf of bread in there.

Now all I had to do was get rid of the idiot in the guard's uniform. Honestly, what kind of a man works in security at a supermarket? Couldn't he get a job with the real police?

I lifted my left hand up and scratched my nose, taking a quick look into the mirror I had taped to my palm. This was another brilliant invention of mine. It meant that I could keep watch behind me without having to turn around. Yep – there he was. Peering at me from around a shelf piled high with eggs.

I'd seen this bloke a few times before. He was older than the other guards employed by this branch – maybe in his forties. He was overweight, too – which meant I could outrun him, if it came to a chase. That didn't mean I fancied running out of here, though. I'd much prefer a casual walk home with my 'purchases'.

I had to lose him.

I waited until a family passed behind me, their trolley piled high with shopping. For a moment, it took me back to the old days. Back to when my…

No, I didn't have time to reminisce. I had to lose the goon in the uniform.

I dropped to my knee and pretended to tie my shoelace – then walked in a stoop at the same speed as the family's shopping trolley. One of their kids watched me with a confused expression on his face.

"I've got a bad back," I said to him with a grin.

A second later, I was able to slip around the side of the vegetable aisle and I was free. I paused to extend my hand mirror past the potatoes and saw the guard looking around in a panic, realising he'd lost sight of me.

Poor sod. I hoped they wouldn't take the cost of what I'd nicked out of his wages.

Acting as calmly as I could, I strolled towards the exit.

As I approached the security scanners by the door, I felt myself tense up a little. Despite the tin foil lining in my bag, there was always the possibility that I'd torn the lining a little when I'd dropped one of my purchases inside, and that the alarms would go off. I readied myself to run at the first sound of them.

Nothing. Yes! The bag was working perfectly. Now I just had to cross the car park and I'd be home free.

"Oi! You!"

I turned to see the security guard racing out of the supermarket behind me. He must have seen me as I'd made for the door. Damn!

Swinging my bag over my shoulder, I broke into a run, making for the gap in the fence behind one of the trolley bays. The hole led to a patch of waste ground at the back of the estate. Once I was there, I'd be able to get away easily enough.

I lifted my hand mirror to check on my pursuer, and was surprised to see how close he was getting. He was fast for his size!

I reached the gap in the fence and tossed my bag through. Then I dropped to my hands and knees to crawl to freedom. I'd almost made it when the security guard grabbed hold of my ankle.

"Get back here!" he snarled.

For a moment, I almost kicked the guard away in an effort to be free – but then I remembered some of the best advice I'd ever been given. "If you fight back, they'll get you for assault as well as shoplifting, and that's far more serious."

Good tip, that. I didn't want to spend a night in the cells charged with attacking this poor fella. He was only doing his job, after all. So I went straight to plan B – distraction...

As the security guard tried to drag me back through the hole in the fence, I reached into my bag and pulled out the jar of pasta sauce I'd just nicked. Lying back to get the best angle, I tossed it over the fence.

SMASH!

The jar smashed to the ground right beside the guard, making him jump and briefly let go of my ankle. This was my chance. I scrambled to my feet, grabbed my bag, and ran onto the waste ground.

This time, I turned rather than using my mirror and grinned at the sight of the guard trying to squeeze his way through my escape hole. It wasn't happening.

"I'll get you next time, you little monster!" he roared after me.

No, I thought. *You won't, mate.*

I didn't stop running until I reached an alley part-way into the estate and I spotted a female figure waiting with her own bag at the other end. It was the person who'd given me that good advice.

"I thought you weren't coming, Joe!" she said with a grin. "Thought you'd been caught."

"No chance," I said. "Slippery as an eel, me." I eyed the other bag with interest. "What did you get?"

My fellow shoplifter opened her bag and I studied her haul – two packets of minced beef, a few cans of cola, and... what was that at the bottom? It couldn't be! A laptop! That would bring in a few quid.

"Yes!" I said, offering a high-five. "Nice one, Mum!"

CHAPTER 2

JOB HUNT

Before we go any further, I want to get a few things straight...

My mum and me – we're not bad people.
Yes, we have to go on the rob for food, and for stuff we can sell to pay the bills. But that's not our fault.

It's my dad's.

We used to be a happy family. We had a nice house, a nice car – and we even went on holiday every year. Nowhere posh like Spain, or whatever, just to a cottage in Cornwall – but it was always brilliant. My dad even bought me a surfboard one year so I could have a go at hitting the waves. Honest to God – a proper surfboard!

Then, he met *her*.

Liz.

She worked at the place where my dad was the manager – a company that printed menus for restaurants and takeaways. If you've had one of those pushed through your letterbox recently, chances are it was printed at my dad's work.

My dad and Liz started to have an affair behind my mum's back. Actually, that's a bit of a joke. He was so rubbish at hiding where he'd been and who he'd been with that he got found out almost straight away.

He wasn't a very good actor, my dad.

I remember the night it all kicked off as though it was yesterday. He came home late from work, saying they'd had to reprint some pizza delivery menus in a hurry because they'd spotted a couple of spelling mistakes. He said he wasn't hungry after staring at pictures of pizzas all evening long. He just wanted to have a bath and go to bed.

So he dumped his wallet and his keys on the side just like always, and went upstairs to run his bath. Only the idiot left the receipt from his hotel room there, without thinking. The hotel room he'd been at all evening with... *her*.

My dad was already in the bath when my mum found the receipt and confronted him with it. He confessed everything, there and then. I sat at the bottom of the stairs, listening to the bathwater splash onto the floor as my parents yelled and screamed at each other.

My dad walked out the next day.

No, that's too simple a way of putting it...

My dad destroyed us the next day.

He left to go and live with Liz, and took everything with him. The TV, the DVD player, the car – and all the savings he and my mum had in their joint bank account.

He left us with nothing.

My mum tried to make the best of it, telling me we were better off without him – but I think she was trying to convince herself as much as me. She tried to get a job, but she hadn't worked since she'd fallen downstairs and hurt her back when I was a toddler, and she really struggled to find anything. In the end, she was taken on as a cleaner in an office block on the other side of town. By the time she'd paid for her bus fare there and back, there wasn't much left, but at least she was doing something positive.

Then, the bank repossessed our house.

While my mum had been looking for work, she'd fallen behind on paying the mortgage, and my dad wasn't coughing up anything to help. My mum went round to Liz's house more than once to try and get him to man-up and pay his fair share, but it fell on deaf ears.

My mum and me ended up in a hostel for the homeless, and that's where we've been ever since. It's not too bad, I guess. We've got our own room, and we're not on the same floor as the drunks. But there's a lot of noise at night, and the police are called to a fight at least once a week, but we do our best to keep ourselves to ourselves.

The really sad part was that my mum lost her job not long after we moved in here. The bosses accused her of stealing a printer from one of the offices. A printer? What the hell would we need one of those for? Still, it didn't matter in the end. They fired her, and that was that.

She signed on for benefits, but we weren't entitled to much at all. I remember sitting in our room one evening, picking the bits of meat out of a supermarket own-brand ready-meal when she said that she wished she *had* stolen that printer. At least that way she could have sold it and bought us a decent dinner.

It was a joke, of course. At least, I thought it was. But, the next night, I came home from school to find fish and chips waiting for me on the table. Not the cook-your-own kind, either – proper fish and chips with salt and vinegar, from the chippy! I hadn't tasted anything so delicious in months.

At first, my mum didn't want to tell me where she'd got the money for them but, in the end, she confessed that she'd nicked an X-Box game from the shop on the corner and sold it to some bloke in the local pub for ten pounds.

I didn't know what to think. My mum and dad had always brought me up to be honest and not to steal other people's belongings. But we were desperate, my mum said, and big shops had insurance policies for stuff that was stolen. The game she'd taken didn't actually belong to anyone, yet. Not really.

I could tell she was trying to convince herself again.

It wasn't long before I was going out with her to nick stuff. Unlike my dad, I've always been pretty good at drama, and it was my job to fall to the floor and pretend I was ill. While the shop staff gathered round to see what was wrong with me, she'd fill her bag with stuff. We always took food at first, because there was no way they could trace empty containers back to you. But, before long, we were also nicking stuff my mum could sell to her contacts in the local pubs and clubs.

We got caught – just the once – as the staff helped me up to my feet and double-checked again that my mum didn't want them to call an ambulance for me. The shop manager came out of the office saying he'd seen my mum putting stuff in her bag on the security camera. The police were called, and we were taken to the station for questioning.

Thankfully, my mum managed to convince them that the sight of me collapsing had made her feel confused and light-headed, and that she hadn't meant to steal anything. As neither of us had a criminal record, they let us go with a caution. I knew they'd be watching out for us in future, so we always went shoplifting separately after that.

And now, here I was, browsing the Internet on a laptop my mum had stolen that afternoon. She hadn't found a buyer for it yet, so I figured I might as well enjoy it while it was there.

I managed to break into the broadband account for the taxi company next door, and then I sat back and wondered what to do next. Aside from the occasional project at school, I hadn't been on the Internet for over a year, ever since we'd had the phone cut off at our old house. It was no good checking emails or logging into Facebook – I didn't have accounts like the rest of my mates. So I started to read through the classified ad listings on local websites. Maybe I could find someone who wanted to buy this laptop and save my mum the bother.

I was about halfway down the list of messages when I spotted it. There, hidden in among the pleas for the return of lost cats, and the people trying to sell off their old lawnmowers, was the ad that would change our lives forever.

I almost missed it at first. It was written in plain text, with no pictures or bold fonts to make it stand out. But what it said blew me away.

Two-man team required for one-off job.
£10,000 fee. No questions asked.

Tel: 0111 494 81254

Ten thousand pounds!

That would really solve our problems! It would mean we could leave the hostel and move into a flat of our own. Mum could get a little car and not have to struggle on the bus if she got a new job.

I grabbed one of the mobile phones I'd nicked from the supermarket from where I'd left it on charge, and rifled through the draw in my bedside table for a SIM card. There had been a rep for some phone company giving them away for free in the shopping centre a few weeks ago. I'd taken a handful, thinking they might come in useful one day. I guess I was right.

I snapped the SIM card into the phone and dialed the number in the ad with trembling hands. The call was answered after three rings.

"Hello?"

"I'm... I'm calling about your ad. You've got a job you need doing?"

A pause, then...

"That's right. You think you can handle it?"

I tried to sound tough. "I can handle anything."

"That's good," said the voice on the phone. "Because I want you to kidnap my daughter."

CHAPTER 3

CAR PARK

I stood in the shadows of the car park and gripped my mum's hand tightly. I was wearing my hoodie, and she had a scarf covering her face. This is where the voice on the 'phone had told us to meet him, and I didn't want him to get a good look at us. Not after what he'd told me his 'little job' was all about.

My mum hadn't been keen when I told her about my call, but the prospect of ten thousand pounds in the bank eventually persuaded her that this was worth doing, despite the risks.

After a few minutes, a sleek, expensive car eased its way into the parking spot beside us. A man in a well-cut suit and long overcoat climbed out of the back. He was older than I had expected – in his mid to late fifties perhaps – and he had thick, black hair which was greased back. A diamond ring sparkled in the dim light.

"Are you Roger?" he asked in a gruff voice.

I nodded. I hadn't used my real name when I'd called him. I'm not stupid.

He looked my mum and me up and down in our scruffy jeans, trainers and sweatshirts. I suddenly felt very, very poor.

"Are you sure you can handle this?"

I took a step forwards, and tried my best to look tall and mean, which wasn't easy as I only came up to this guy's chest.

"We can handle it," I said. "You got the money?"

The man paused, then pulled a plain envelope from his jacket pocket. "£5,000 now, £5,000 later."

"Sounds fair," I said, taking the envelope and sliding it into my own pocket. I really hoped he couldn't tell that my hand was shaking. I'd never held so much money in one go before.

The man reached back into the car and produced a folder. On the front was a picture of a girl of eleven or twelve years old. "This is my daughter, Tiffany," he said. "Inside you'll find details of where she goes to school, how she gets there and what she does in her spare time."

I glanced down at the girl in the picture. It was a school photo. She had long, blonde hair, tied into pigtails.

"I don't want to know how you're going to do it, or when," said the man, handing over the folder. "That's up to you. Just make sure you call the number when you've got her."

"No problem," I said. "We won't let you down."

The man turned to get back into his car, when my mum spoke out for the first time.

"Why are you doing this?"

The man slowly turned back to face us. "The ad said 'no questions'," he growled.

"I know," said my mum. "But – your own daughter..."

Another pause, longer this time. When he spoke again, his voice sounded harder.

"You remember that boy who was kidnapped while he was on holiday with his family in Greece last year? It was all over the news."

Mum nodded. "I remember."

"The public was horrified by the crime," said the man. "Horrified to the point of rushing to donate money into a fund to help his devastated parents find their little angel. They got over five million pounds in the first week alone."

"And you want to do the same with Tiffany?" asked my mum. "You're going to sit there on TV, crying and asking people to help find her so that you can line your own pockets?"

"You're starting to sound very virtuous for someone who's just taken ten grand to kidnap an innocent little girl," the man rumbled.

I stepped in. "We've only got five grand."

The man snarled. "I told you – you'll get the rest when you've got Tiffany."

He got into his car without another word. He nodded to his driver and they drove away, leaving us standing in the shadows. I felt the bulge of the money stuffed into my pocket and realised that we were now deeply involved in a crime far more serious than nicking a few DVDs from the local supermarket.

Now, we just had to figure out how to do it.

CHAPTER 4

THE HARD WAY

We studied Tiffany's file for the next two days. The school she went to was a private facility where the well-off sent their kids to be educated away from, well... away from the likes of me, I suppose.

A couple of nights a week, she stayed behind after classes to either play hockey or to practise her show-jumping. She even had a horse of her own, a pale-brown thing called Chestnut that was kept in an exclusive stables on the outskirts of town.

That's where we decided to make our move.

My mum rented a van with the money we now had, and we parked it part-way down the track leading to Chestnut's stables. We were both dressed in farmer-type clothes, and my mum was writing something on a clipboard. Then, at exactly the time we'd been promised in her file, Tiffany came walking along the lane, carrying her riding helmet.

My mum jumped out of the van. "Sorry," she called out, waving her clipboard, "you can't go any further, I'm afraid. There's been an accident at the stable yard."

I was hiding at the back of the van, so I couldn't see Tiffany, but I could hear the panic in her voice.

"Accident?" she cried. "What kind of accident?"

"Some idiot fell asleep at the wheel of his Landrover and ploughed into the stables. One of the horses was badly injured. The vet is there now, putting it to sleep."

Tiffany gasped. "Which horse?"

My mum looked down the list she pretended to have on her clipboard. "Let me see... ah, here it is. A light brown eight-year-old called Chestnut."

I almost felt sorry for Tiffany. She gave out a strangled sob and ran past my mum in the direction of the stables. As she stumbled past me, tears already flowing down her cheeks, I pulled a sack down over her head and pushed her into the back of the van.

"Go! Go!" I shouted over Tiffany's muffled screams.

My mum jumped into the driver's seat, as I jumped in beside Tiffany and closed the van doors. Within a few minutes, we were driving back towards our part of town.

I cautiously pulled the sack from Tiffany's head. "Don't make a noise, and we promise not to hurt you," I said.

Tiffany nodded, but then obviously changed her mind. "Help!" she bellowed as we pulled up at a set of traffic lights. "Help me!"

I grabbed a roll of tape and tore off a strip. "Now we've got to do things the hard way," I said, pressing the tape over her mouth and ripping off another strip for her wrists.

Back at the hostel, we waited until it was dark, then bundled Tiffany into our room. Once inside, I sat her on my bed and grabbed the mobile phone and dialled.

"It's done," I said as the same, brooding voice answered the call.

"Prove it," came the response.

I went over to Tiffany and carefully pulled the tape from her mouth, but left her wrists taped together behind her back. "Say your name and where you are," I commanded, holding the phone up to her ear.

"M... my name is Tiffany King," she sobbed, "and I don't know where I am. Two people grabbed me near the stables and they've brought me to some cheap hotel."

"That's enough!" I snapped, pulling the phone away. My mum moved in to place a fresh strip of tape over Tiffany's mouth.

"When do we get the rest of the money?" I demanded into the mobile.

"Patience," said the man with a low chuckle. "Let's get the donations coming in from well-wishers first."

"That wasn't the agreement..." I began, but all I could hear was the dial tone.

Tiffany's father had hung up.

I dropped the mobile beside the laptop on my bedside table and stood with my mum as she studied our prisoner.

"What now?" my mum asked, guessing the call hadn't gone well.

I shrugged. "We wait."

CHAPTER 5

CHILD'S PLAY

The next few days were a nightmare.
Mum and I took it in turns to sleep in her bed,
while Tiffany slept in mine. We fed our prisoner
and gave her drinks, each time making her
promise not to scream before taking the tape
from her mouth.

Using the toilet was the worst. We didn't have
our own bathroom at the hostel; we had to
use the shared facilities at the end of the hall.
Whenever Tiffany needed to pee, we had to
check that the coast was clear while my mum
hurried down to the bathroom with her. I stood
outside the door, keeping watch, then giving

three knocks to signal that no one was around and we could take her back to the room.

I tried calling the number of our employer several times, but no one answered.

As we didn't have a TV in our room, we watched news updates online on the laptop. The kidnapping of Tiffany King was the big story on every channel, with reporters stationed outside her school, her home and on the track leading down to Chestnut's stables.

On the third day, Tiffany's parents gave a press conference, begging for whoever had taken their little girl to please let her go. Her dad hardly looked like the man we'd met in the dark car park to take on the job. Instead of the strong, slightly scary man we'd faced, here he was in jumper and jeans, crying for the release of his daughter. He was a much better actor than my dad.

And then, just as had been predicted, the news reported that a fund was being set up to help in the search for Tiffany. A number appeared on the screen and, from all over the country, people started to donate. They hit £125,000 in the first twenty-four hours.

Tiffany sat and watched all the news reports with us, barely showing any emotion – until she saw the distress her mum was in during the press conference. Mum grabbed a tissue from her handbag and gently wiped away our hostage's tears.

That night, as I finished feeding Tiffany a chicken korma from the takeaway on the corner, she looked straight into my eyes. "Please don't put the tape back over my mouth," she said. "I promise I won't make any noise."

I glanced over at my mum, who nodded.

"OK," I said, "but if you try anything..."

"I won't," Tiffany promised.

I stuffed the takeaway cartons into a plastic bag and left it near the door to throw out in the morning.

"Why are you doing this?" Tiffany asked quietly.

Neither my mum nor I, spoke. We didn't know what to say.

"If you need money, contact my dad," said Tiffany. "He's rich. He'll give you whatever you want. Just let me go."

"It's not as simple as that," I said.

"Of course it is," countered Tiffany. "It's a straight exchange. You've got me, and he's got money."

"Not enough, according to him," said my mum. "At least, not yet."

I froze, praying that Tiffany hadn't heard what she had said – but, of course, she had.

"What do you mean?" our prisoner asked, her brow furrowing.

"Nothing," said my mum. "I made a mistake."

"No," said Tiffany. "You said my dad didn't have enough money yet, according to him. What do you mean?"

I sighed, and sat down beside her.

I don't know whether it was the pressure of being cooped up in this horrible room for the past few days, or the growing worry that, instead of giving us our outstanding £5,000, Tiffany's dad was going to blame us for the kidnapping – but I told her everything. How her dad had placed the ad online, how he'd paid us to grab her, and how he wanted the public to pay millions into a fund to find her and make him richer than ever.

When I had finished, Tiffany sat in silence, staring down at the threadbare cover on my duvet. Eventually, she spoke in a low whisper.

"I hate him!"

I struggled to hold back a laugh, but obviously not well enough. Tiffany's head snapped up and she glared at me.

"You think this is funny?" she spat.

"Not at all," I admitted. "In fact, I'm terrified. I just never thought that you and me would ever have something in common."

It was Tiffany's turn to laugh. She glanced around the dump my mum and I called home. "I very much doubt that," she said.

So I told her about my dad. About how he'd left us for a girl at work, and how we'd had to turn to shoplifting to make ends meet.

"Shoplifting?" she said when I'd finished. "Child's play! I was shoplifting by the time I was six years old!" She leaned across the bed to me, eyes sparkling. "Have you ever tried hacking?"

"Well, I cracked the wi-fi password of the taxi company next door," I said.

"Noob!" cried Tiffany with a grin. "Untie my wrists and I'll show you some real hacking..."

I hesitated, and glanced at my mum.

"Oh, come on!" said Tiffany. "I've just found out that my dad arranged for me to be kidnapped – and you know he's going to let you take the fall for this, don't you?"

"I'd more or less figured out as much," I said.

"Then what say we get back at both our dads?"

That, I couldn't resist. I grabbed a pair of scissors from the drawer and cut through the tape holding Tiffany's wrists behind her back. Mum stood near the door in case our hostage took the opportunity for a break for freedom but, instead, she grabbed the laptop and entered the address of an élite London bank into the browser.

"My dad changes his online banking password at least once a week," Tiffany explained as she worked. "He's paranoid that someone will break in and steal from him. Shame he doesn't know that's how his little princess here has been funding her horse-loving lifestyle for years..."

I couldn't help but smile as I watched Tiffany's fingers fly across the keys. She quickly opened a second browser window and downloaded a small piece of software, into which she typed her dad's bank account number. She hit 'enter', and the program began to cycle through possible passwords, based on those he had used in the past and mentions of the family in the press. Then...

PING!

"Got it!" exclaimed Tiffany. "This week's password is... KIDNAP. Oh, Dad – you're so predictable."

A few seconds later, Tiffany was inside her dad's bank account. "No alarms, as we logged in with the correct password," she said, "and as I'm surfing from behind a proxy server, this laptop cannot be traced."

My mum and I exchanged an impressed smile.

"Now," said Tiffany, cracking her knuckles. "How much did my dad offer you?"

"Ten thousand," said my mum. "But he only gave us five."

"Then I reckon you deserve at least thirty," said Tiffany.

"Thirty thousand pounds!" cried my mum.

"Let's make it forty," said Tiffany. "You did have to feed me, after all. I'll transfer it into one of my secret, off-shore bank accounts first, then I'll set up a similar account for you to access it. That way, we won't raise any suspicions."

"Won't your dad be angry?" I asked.

Tiffany beamed. "He'll be furious. But knowing the way he makes his money – through dodgy stuff like this – he hasn't got anything to complain about."

"What about you?" I asked.

"Are you kidding?" said Tiffany. "Little posh girl is kidnapped on the orders of her uncaring father? I'll be on TV chat shows for weeks! I might even get a book deal out of it!"

PING!

"There!" she said. "You're now forty thousand pounds richer!"

I ran across the room and hugged my mum. Our worries were over!

"Now," said Tiffany. "Let's see about your dad..."

CHAPTER 6

YOU HAVE THE RIGHT...

Mum and I crouched behind a stack of boxes containing printed kebab menus, and watched. In the office above the factory floor, the light was on in my dad's office – but he wasn't working late. We could hear Liz giggling up there with him. They were having a great time.

Down below, taped to a wooden chair beside one of the now-silent printing machines, sat Tiffany. I hadn't wanted to tape her mouth closed again, but she had insisted.

"We have to make this look authentic," she said.

So I pressed a strip of tape across her mouth and pulled the sack down over her head.

Then I made the call.

The police smashed in through the front doors of the factory less than fifteen minutes later.

"Police!"

"Show yourselves!"

"Come out with your hands in the air!"

The office door swung open and my dad stepped out, his shirt unbuttoned to the waist. I felt my mum tense up beside me, so I squeezed her hand.

"What's going on?" my dad demanded.

"Hands where I can see them!" ordered an armed officer, his gun trained up the staircase. "Come down, slowly."

Liz appeared in the doorway. "Jerry?"
she squeaked.

"You too!" roared the police officer.
"Downstairs, now!"

Then, one of the policemen spotted Tiffany.
He ran over and pulled the sack from her head.
Tears were rolling down her cheeks. She was just
as good an actor as me!

"Are you Tiffany King?"

Tiffany nodded, dumbly.

"We've got her!" the officer yelled.

As my dad and Liz reached the bottom of the
staircase, Tiffany screamed. "That's them!" she
sobbed, pointing to the bemused couple. "Those
are the two people who kidnapped me!"

"What!" exclaimed my dad. "No, that's not true!"

"I'd know them anywhere!" Tiffany continued.

"They work for my dad. He's the one that paid them to grab me. Look into his bank account – he's bound to have made some sort of secret payment to them!"

Oh, Tiffany was good!

A sergeant spoke into his radio. "Can we arrange an arrest warrant for Mr Desmond King, and let's have a search warrant for his personal accounts while we're at it. I think he has a couple of questions to answer."

More police officers appeared. They turned my dad and Liz to face the wall and began to search them. "You are under arrest for the abduction of Miss Tiffany King," one of them said as he worked. "You have the right to remain silent, but anything you do say may be taken down and given in evidence against you."

"But, we haven't done anything!" my dad insisted as he was handcuffed.

"That's it," whispered my mum in my ear. "I've seen enough."

As Tiffany had a blanket wrapped around her shoulders, me and my mum crept towards the fire exit we'd left open when we first arrived. Tiffany spotted us leaving our hiding place and, when she was sure none of the police were watching her, she winked at me.

The cold night air washed over us as we stepped out into the moonlight. "Forty grand in the bank, and this..." I said, pulling what was left of our initial fee from my pocket. "There's just under four thousand there, I reckon. So, what first? Our own flat, or a new car?"

"Neither!" grinned my mum, linking her arm through mine. "I fancy a holiday – anywhere but Cornwall!"

THE END